After
Party

Ci James

The Leaving Party

Life had whizzed past her. The black shells of wood blurred past the led sky; the hollow houses disappeared in the dust; the grey mist whipped at the windows. A tunnel sucked up the carriage. Darkness. Bria's fingers skimmed the surface of the glass. The wheels roared underneath the floors. A dim overhead light flickered as she read.

'Well, I never..' said the man next to her.

'What?'

The train rocked gently.

'I never thought I'd see someone read again.'

The man leaned over, straining at the portable screen she held in her wrinkled hands. Bria looked at the man's old, drawn face. His thin, blue lips were carved into a curious smile and a sparkle of youth still glittered in his eyes.

'Reading is a good way to stay distracted,' said Bria, entertaining his eagerness.

The man leaned closer, lowering his gaze.

'What is it about?'

'The archives call it cli-fi.'

'You mean sci-fi.'

'No,' frowned Bria. 'Cli-fi.'

She took advantage of his pause.

'Climate fiction. It's a very old genre, you see.' She pointed at the date on the first page. The man gasped.

'And what is climate fiction?' He questioned. 'Does the writer imagine a eutopia of harmless weather? Warm, summer mornings and frosty winter nights?'

The old face returned to the back of his seat and smiled faintly. A reminiscent warmth glazed over him.

'At least, that's what my grandparents talked about when they mentioned the weather.'

Bria nodded. She spoke quietly while taking in his sensitive expression.

'This book was written when the weather was just like that. The writer imagined a future of scorching summers and baron winters. Immigration, famine, war, and finally emptiness.' She looked away. 'Life as we know it now.'

'So, it was a prophecy?'

'It was a scientific prediction.'

She snapped the device away and watched the walls of the tunnel rush away.

'It's miserable, I know, to think how easy it once was.'

'It'll be over soon,' smiled the man. A hungry grin opened up across his face.

Bria looked uneasily around her. The tunnels felt emptier and the light was harder. Who wanted to openly acknowledge it? She went back to reading and the man spoke again.

'Reading is a good distraction,' he chuckled.

Her frail eyes averted from the page and the quiet voice betrayed fear.

'It feels morbid. This journey.'

'Think of it as a symbol. Like going to your own funeral but you get to go home at the end of it.'

Bria bit her lip. 'The leaving celebration makes it feel very official.'

'It's better to celebrate while the rest of us are still alive. Most of won't have long left.'

The man's tone startled Bria. She sat back suddenly and inhaled sharply. The walls of the tunnel flapped away and the carriage filled with bleak daylight. Outside looked even emptier than before.

-

Bria was lost under the crisp blue sky. There were hundreds of people who had joined her. She was just another wrinkled, fleshy face amongst the frail skeletons, drifting like a pale leaf. The forest was a portrait of wooden spindly sticks mapped across the sky.

'Funny thing is the sky looks cleaner,' said the same man from the train.

'What do you mean?'

'Even in the middle of an apocalypse, the sky looks cleaner.' He said again. 'I've seen photos of the past and they had these big smoky white trails stripped across the sky. Airplanes moving back and fourth pumping poison into the atmosphere. And now look at it.'

The man pointed a spindly finger up through the cracks in the trees. 'Crisp, blue sky,' he smiled. 'I'm going to miss it.'

He suddenly stopped and put his hand out.

'You hear that?' he whispered, 'Do you hear that?'

Bria listened closely and her stomach churned.

'It's water,' said the man. His face filled with wonder. 'Look, look.'

His creaking bones and tired skin burst into life, as if rays of warm sunlight had instantly bathed his cold body. The man diverted gently from the crowd and looked downwards at a slope. It was six feet down.

'Quick,' he ushered. 'Who knows when we'll see this again.'

He started to slide down and Bria reluctantly took his hand as they staggered toward it. When they reached the bottom of the slope they arrived at a glistening blue stream.

'Beautiful, isn't it?'

The water flowed mindlessly. It had no idea that humanity was coming to an end and it didn't care. When humans were dead the water would carry on its journey. Light bounced off of the surface and exploded like white stars. He picked up a pebble and threw it against the water. It skipped across the distance and left rippling halos in its dust.

'Look at that,' said the man. 'My old man taught me that as a kid. I can still do it.'

Bria was hypnotised by the silver ripples and the bobbing movement of the water. The man's voice became so distant that it sounded like she was in a tunnel. She looked at the water, setting her eyes into the water, deeper and deeper.

-

Bria dabbed her lip with a trembling thumb. The dark shade of red lipstick melted into her mouth. The cold, blue winter had drawn itself across the sky. Frost glistened across the lawn. Bria sat in the quiet living room with dazed, frightened eyes. The fireplace crackled and she watched the front window. She was 40 years younger. The world was younger.

Her eyes focused beyond the window. Waiting for him. Jalen knew. She was almost certain that he'd set his spies on her and that they would have reported it back to him in prison. It didn't matter how hard she had tried to hide the bump on her belly, someone would have seen it. And Jalen would have known. She was pregnant.

A scrawny, dark figure trampled forward from the distance and Bria held her breath. She cradled the bump and then quickly released it. Keys jangled behind the wooden door and then it clicked into place. She breathed.

For a while she didn't look ahead at the front door. She stared blankly out at the window, eyeing the river that drifted dully beyond the house. She felt his shadow stretch across the floor.

'So it's true.' He said, looking down at her.

Jalen's face was molten red. His long, curly black hair was dusted in a sprinkling of snow from outside.

'Jalen..' she said quietly.

'Don't get up,' he grunted. He stared at her stomach.'How could you do this to me? To yourself? You know that children are not the future.'

Jalen stood still and averted his eyes into the dancing fire.

'I have spent months in prison, Bria. They called me a terrorist.'

Bria's eyes were swelling with tears. Her throat was tight.

'When I joined the organisation, nobody cared. Just another crazy activist. But then people started listening. And gradually society did what was best for this planet. They stopped having children. And then when people started listening, I was a threat. We're a cancer to this planet, Bria. Why would you bring a child into it? I thought that we understood each other.'

'I don't know, Jalen. It wasn't deliberate, Jalen. It's yours. It's your baby.'

'You'll be bringing a baby into a hostile world. Droughts, blistering heat, mass migration, famines, wars. What a cruel thing to do!'

A tear slid down Bria's cheek.

'You had a choice Bria. You still have a choice.' He took a deep breath and lowered his voice to a deathly grunt. 'You can still get rid of it. This thing didn't ask to be born. You'll bring it into this world without a choice because of your weak, sentimental attachment. It'll look at up at you one day and wonder why you brought it into this world. And what are you going to tell it?'

Her body quivered.

'You want to keep it' His eyes darted off under a trance. 'I think I understand. You want to keep it because abortions are illegal now. You're afraid of prison, that's it, right?'

He looked away from the various corners of the ceiling and set his cold eyes upon her. She felt the walls close in and his dry voice squeezed her body tight.

'You didn't abort because you were frightened. But you will get rid of it when it has been born, won't you?'

Bria tried to speak but her body wretched.

'That's right..' he rambled to himself. 'You'll get rid of it after it's born. There's a river outside. We'll drown it then. I'm here for you now, Bria. We'll drown it together, won't we?'

-

Bria moved her eyes away from the stream. The man from the train had been talking but the words has washed over her.

'My old man would have been proud to know that I can still skip a stone like that,' he laughed triumphantly. 'What about you, did you have any children?'

Bria's eyes hardened.

'We need to get back to the crowd,' she snapped. 'The leaving party is starting soon.'

Bria and the man from the train clambered back up the hill and then moved towards the party. There were battered signs on sticks pointing them to the celebration. Within a few minutes their speed had caught them back up to the crowd and they had merged back into the crowd. Bria drifted on her feet, focusing her energy into repressing the flashbacks of her memory. She caught herself sliding her hand over her tummy and she immediately pulled it away. When she looked back up, the man from the train had disappeared, lost in the mass, and then a wide, green space opened up.

'Welcome!' announced Cade.

A strong, robust figure emerged on the stage in front of them. He was dressed in the same black, formal attire as hundreds of attendees and a microphone boomed his voice out across the audience. A respectful applause rippled across the forest.

'I'm honoured that so many of you have joined me today,' said Cade proudly. 'what a dignified way to end it.'

The audience clapped again.

'Today we pay our respects to a life lived well. Humanity has done very well.' Cade smirked. 'Today we participate in the final dance.'

Cade pointed his finger randomly into the crowd. She felt like his finger was stabbing her in the chest.

'You will die soon.' Announced Cade. His finger swirled wildly. 'And you. And you. And you. And you.'

He jumped off of the stage and ventured into the crowd. The wire from his microphone trailed behind him like a sliver of oil. His body shook with adrenaline.

'You have accepted it. You know it's coming, and you know that we're on the brink of an extinction. What a privilege that get to celebrate that.'

The quiet, timid Bria was suddenly bewildered to find famous Cade standing in front of her. His smoky breath stung her eyes and his hungry lips hovered closely to his face.

'Are you ready?' he said to her.

Bria trembled. Her throat was dry.

'This poor, nervous lady.' Cade embraced her with his muscly arms. 'This lost child of ours. She has joined the leaving party and she is not ready to leave!'

A roar of disapproval rose from the audience and Bria pushed herself away. The old, decrepit audience roared like an angry mob.

'My child,' said Cade. 'You have one more choice before our species are wiped out. Will you die alone one day? Worried and cold in your house, with no one around you. Or you will you die with your brothers and sisters. Tonight.'

Bria felt her world spin and she stumbled across the grass. The jeers of 'tonight' blasted across the forest. She straightened up and looked into his cold eyes.

'Alone,' she said.

Cade frowned. The crowd plunged into silence.

'My lost child,' said Cade. He spoke warmly into the microphone. 'It's ok to be frightened.'

For a moment the bleak light hit Cade's face and the image of Jalen flashed before her. His long, curly dark hair and menacing eyes cut into her chest, and she found herself pinned to the sofa, just as when Jalen had told her to kill the baby. Bria took a sharp breath.

'I'm not frightened now,' she said defiantly to Cade.

Cade released her and cradled the microphone in both of his hands.

'When I told people to stop having children, the authorities imprisoned me.' Said Cade. 'I was labelled a terrorist. A danger to humanity. And yet, people were starving. The world was hostile. Humans were becoming weak. The heat was smothering us. I knew that this wasn't our home anymore.'

Cade disappeared further into the crowd and his voice filled with fury. As his lips moved Bria struggled to work out whether it was him speaking or the memory of Jalen.

'And then, even with me being locked up, the birth rates still fell. We had overpopulated. And so we shrunk. Day by day. Soon the climate and the chemicals in the air did to us what we couldn't bring ourselves to do. Soon we couldn't have children even if we wanted to.'

Cade's laugh was maniacal.

'It's here, the end of the world as you know it.'

Cade grabbed another unsuspecting member of the audience who shook in his arm.

'And this is why we have gathered today. To wave goodbye. To celebrate what was left.'

Bria observed Cade from the distance. He still moved with fresh precision and his chest moved with

deep, triumphant gasps. The long black hair which had reminded her of Jalen swayed effortlessly with his movement. When he had finished his presentation, he leapt back onto the stage with more youth and vigor than she had seen in years.

'Bring out the drinks!' he announced.

Men and women with skeletal faces marched in from the corners behind the stage. They were carrying small cocktails on silver platters. Some members of the audience lunged for the drinks, while others – including Bria – politely turned away. A steely drizzle fell upon the forest.

Cade looked into the sky and spoke gently into the microphone.

'My brothers and sisters, it has been an honour.' He said.

Bria looked around for the man on the train but she couldn't see him. Cade's farewell speech breezed past her but most of the audience hung on his words. On his command, the audience chugged back on the drinks with choreographed movement like a ballet.

Bria suddenly spotted the man from the train. His eyes faintly caught her from the side. He swung back and swallowed the drink.

The rain was pouring and Bria stood as groans and muttered ramblings flittered across her. Figures collapsed and sunk into the muddy water. The microphone whined as Cade collapsed on the stage with a rumbling thunder. Cocktails glasses shattered and people wretched, vomiting blood at their feet and then falling into the darkness. Shadows disappeared into splashes of water and the rain hammered down at the dead bodies swimming around her. She looked up at the white flashes of lightning and closed her eyes until the forest had grown silent. When she opened her eyes she was alone. Her breathing was drowned out by the hard patter of rain on the ground. Bria looked over at Cade's body scrawled across the stage and she looked down at the corpses across her feet.

I'm not afraid, she repeated to herself desperately. I'm not afraid.

Gender Reveal

I can predict a baby's gender before it is born.

My success rate is 99%. It's a gift, a talent, a social superpower. People love it. They get a real kick out of it. The baby doesn't even have to be kicking.

You probably want to know how I do it. I'll be honest, I don't know how I do it. I just know the gender. It's just.. There. I place my hand over a pregnant woman's tummy and close my eyes. I plunge into darkness and feel my mind collapse into the unknown realm of supernaturalism. A calmness falls upon me like a soft, silk blanket from the ethereal depths of the abyss and I ease into its warmth. I snuggle into that blanket deeper until the image appears. Then I have the answer. It takes about 5 seconds.

'Please,' begs Colette. 'I really want to know.'

'Then wait a few more months,' I say glumly.

'It's just the gender.'

'I don't want to do it to you.' I avoid her gaze. 'It's different, with you.'

We're standing outside a coffee shop on a cold winter's day. The wind raps on our cheeks and sinks into our bones. The early commuters are bustling through us like phantoms.

'It's really cold,' I say. 'Look, snowflakes are falling from the sky.'

The colourless sky hangs above us miserably. White specks of dust fall from it and settle on the pavement.

'It will take you 5 seconds!' she grins. 'What were the chances of us bumping into each other here? It's fate. You believe in that, right? You have to do it!'

'It's not fate,' I say glumly. 'I get coffee here every day. You walk past this place. Our paths have crossed. Big deal.'

'You have a gift.'

I rub my hands together and recoil into my coat.

'It's you. I don't want to do it.'

'Are you upset because we dated? It was years ago. It lasted a month. You can do this for me, right?'

'Colette,' I sigh. 'The accuracy can change if I have any attachment to the person. It's better when there's anonymity.'

She looks at me blankly.

'Ok, sure, I'm weird about it. We had something. We dated. I know you've moved on and I'm sure the father of this child makes you very happy. It's still weird for me.'

'Are you still in love with me?'

'No, no,' I say, waving my hands defensively.

'Good, because, you know, we would never have been anything special,' she smiles.

'And you want me to you a favour?'

She wriggles her nose and her eyes gloss over.

'Alright,' I say. 'Stand closer.'

She steps up until I can feel her warm breath on my face. I place my hand over her bump and close my eyes.

The darkness engulfs me for a few moments. I feel like I am sinking into a sandpit. Usually the answer arrives like a flash of light and then I take my hand away and get on with my life. Something different happens here. I fall further, faster. The sand draws me deep into the core.

Her name is Kendra. She has her Mum's emerald green eyes and wavy, brunette hair. She has her Dad's tanned complexion. I see the floral dress and chubby baby cheeks. Kendra is waddling across a colourful dance floor and disco lights are illuminating the party. Where is she? I feel like a drunken camera man who has started learning how to fly. My eyes hover across the illuminating tiles trying to absorb the scene. She's at a wedding. Baby Kendra is running.. running.. there she is, up to her mother. I see Colette reach down and pick her up in a long, majestic white dress.

I've never seen Colette's boyfriend before and, yet, there he is. Bushy eyebrows and Mediterranean skin. They're getting married. This is a wedding. Colette's wedding! Kendra, how old is she? I strain closer into the faint image. This is a toddler.

Colette looks gorgeous. Just the way she looked when I first met her. There are small dark circles under her eyes and the face has drawn out. Her hair has lost the zest of a lightning blonde flash. But she's still incredible. Her green eyes dazzle me. What a gift, that Kendra has inherited her mother's eyes.

I'm floating around in the abstract world, stumbling through the air. I admire Colette's smile from the distance. A ray of light flickers in the corner of my eyes and suddenly I'm outside.

Kendra is crying and Colette is applying a cream to her daughter's knee. A small, purple bike is lying toppled on the pavement with the wheels still spinning in motion. A crimson sunset melts upon us. Colette's face is serious but gentle. She coos to Kendra and kisses the knee.

'That's life, baby,' she says. 'You fall down and you get back up again.'

Kendra cries some more.

'And this?' she kisses Kendra's cut again. 'This is a magic kiss. It has healing properties.'

Kendra stops crying and looks up at her mother wide shimmering eyes.

'You see?' smiles Colette. 'You'll be okay.. you'll be okay..'

I turn my eyes to Colette and watch a forced smile flicker on the corners of her face. Her eyelashes flutter with tears of her own.

I'm in a kitchen. Colette and Kendra are arguing. Kendra has grown to the same height as her mother. Her frame is slender and her dark, galaxy hair is down to her back. I perch mid air and watch.

'You had me sick with worry!' shouts Colette. 'I didn't know where you were, who you were with!'

'Mum, get over it! I'm 18!'

'You're still living under my roof. You get home when I tell you to!'

'You don't own me!'

'I'm your mother!'

'I hate you! Ever since Dad left you've been a terrible mother!'

Kendra picks up a plate and throws it against the wall. White shards dance across the kitchen like a hailstorm. Broken chunks of the plate fall straight through me.

'Kendra, stop it!' pleads Colette.

Colette recoils and sinks into the back of wall. Kendra stomps out of the kitchen and her mother calls out to her.

'Where are you going?'

'Away from you!'

I watch Colette slide onto the floor and whimper quietly. I try to reach out to her but I'm just a cameraman. When I try to say something the room is still quiet.

I'm in the backseat of a car. Kendra is nervously holding the driver's wheel and Colette has her hand wrapped firmly around the hand break.

'It's okay to make mistakes,' says Colette.

'I can't do this, I'm never going to pass this test,' shakes Kendra.

We're perched by the road on a quiet residential area. An empty roundabout looms in front of Kendra.

'I hate roundabouts,' says Kendra.

'You can do this,' smiles Collette.

Colette steps out of the car and starts to check the tyres. I pass through the passenger doors and watch her examine the car. She carries herself with a newfound confidence; a steely independence in her tense shoulders.

'The wheels are ok,' she says leaning into the passenger window. 'You only nudged the curb. That's the only way you're going to learn, by making mistakes. In a few months you'll have passed your driver's test and this whole thing will seem like a distant memory to you.'

Kendra steps out of the car and takes a deep breath of the early morning air.

'I can't even afford to drive. I don't think it's worth it.'

'I'm paying for your first test, remember?' says Colette. 'I want you to be independent in life.'

Kendra shakes her head. Her brown hair swishes with the rapid movement.

'Not worth it.'

'Do you think I enjoy teaching someone to drive?' says Colette. 'I'm doing this for you. I want you to have your independence. I don't want you to rely on people.'

The pair stand quietly opposite the car. Kendra looks down at the road and a cold breeze breathes over them.

'Get back in the car,' says Colette after a while.

Kendra is even older now. She's laughing with her Mum. They've cosied up on a sofa by a fireplace and Kendra is scooping out Vanilla ice cream.

'I always thought there was something odd that boyfriend of yours,' says Colette as she strokes her daughter's hair.

Kendra is a little older now. Her eyes are bloodshot and cheeks puffy. Colette's hair is bright blonde again. Her jawline has become a little harder and the lines under her eyes have thickened. She has aged with grace. Maybe she looks even better as an older woman.

'Thank you, Mother,' says Kendra. 'You know how to make me feel better. Since the breakup things have been so hard.'

'Breakups are hard,' comforts Kendra. 'You know, before I dated your father, I was with this guy I met at school. We only dated for a month. He became famous. He could tell the gender of a baby just by touching a woman's tummy.'

'Was he a magician?'

'No, although he was like one.' She stops and dreamily reminisces. 'I wondered if I could fall in love with him. Never told him. He was quite young and didn't know what he wanted in life. I wanted to have a family. We were different moved on. I never quite forgot about him though.'

Kendra looks up and rolls her eyes.

'Alright, whatever.'

I can hear of cracking in the fireplace. Their shadows dance wildly against a beige wall.

'Do you want to get married again?'

Colette's eyes turn cold for a moment, and then a small smile broadens across her face.

'I already have the love of my life. I have you. If I die without a man I don't care. You are all that I want.'

Kendra closes her eyes and then sinks into her mother's arms. I feel a teardrop slide down my cheek.

I'm at another wedding. I'm sitting next to Colette on a big, frilly white table. The room is surrounded by unfamiliar faces. Kendra is walking around in a wedding dress. Her shoes click against the marble floor.

'You must be really proud of her,' I say to Colette. She doesn't hear me, of course.

Kendra is dancing around with a white grin on her face. Her hair swishes in the party and her friends are dancing around her in colourful dresses.

'I got married in this same place,' smiles Colette to another woman next to her. 'I can't believe the place is still standing.'

'Your daughter looks very happy. You must be really proud.'

Colette smiles and lots of wrinkles form around her face. Her hair has sharp lines of silver piercing through the blonde. Her back is arched. The emerald eyes dazzle from afar.

Kendra walks over and hugs her mother.

'How are you feeling?'

'I'm okay,' says Colette weakly.

Kendra's face wavers with anxiety.

'Do you want me to take you home? Are you in pain?'

'Please,' smiles Colette. 'Enjoy your day. There's nothing wrong with me.'

'The doctor advised that if you..'

Colette closes her eyes and looks away.

'I'm not going anywhere. Enjoy your day, Kendra.'

Kendra kisses Colette gently on the cheek and then strokes her bony hand. Kendra walks back to the dancefloor and Colette watches from a far. After a few seconds the elderly woman's eyes arch and her lips tremble. She looks at the floor and she smiles to herself.

The room darkens. A grey veil falls over it and the walls cave in on me. I'm in a bedroom. Colette is laying down on a bed with Kendra sitting next to her. Colette is frail. Her face is hollow and the hair has gone. The emeralds are flickering.

'Please,' sobs Kendra, 'don't leave yet.'

Colette can't say anything. She reaches out her skeletal hand and holds her daughter's shaking fingers. Colette takes deep breaths like she has broken the finish line of a marathon. Finally she speaks.

'I know you can make a success of yourself without me,' croaks Colette. 'You've made me so proud. I know you'll live a fantastic life without me.'

Kendra cries and kisses her mother's bony hand. With a few more deep breaths, Colette slowly closes her eyes and stops breathing.

'Well?'

I open my eyes and take a deep breath of cold air. Snow flakes are falling around me. I'm outside a coffee shop and Colette is standing in front of me. My hand is on her tummy.

'That has to have been at least a minute now! What is it? A girl or a boy?'

I remove my hand and stutter wildly. I look at Colette's young, fresh face.

'Did you see the gender?'

I withdraw back into my coat.

'Her name is Kendra,' I say slowly.

Colette looks at me with a dizzy, hopeful smile.

'Her name is Kendra.' I say it with deep a breath. 'And she'll make you very happy.'

Erin

'It sounds like the ocean is outside,' said Erin.

The group of boys laughed. They were all sitting on a cozy, checkered bed with layers of black and white covers. Erin was leaning on the back of the head board with her knees up to her chest and her timid face sinking into her teal jumper.

'What has Erin been smoking?' said one of the boys.

She closed her eyes and a warm smile spread across her face.

'It's here,' she protested softly. Her eyes twinkled. 'The ocean is here.'

'I want to be where she is,' said another one of the guys. He took a drag of smoke. 'Erin, baby, we're nowhere near the ocean. We're on the 15th floor. Your place.'

She laughed and shook her head. The bob of short brown hair swished across her face like ripples in a stream.

'Another smoke?' said the same boy, handing a smoking joint to her.

'I think she has had enough,' interrrupted the first guy.

He held out his arm and drew it across Erin like a drawbridge.

'Erin, baby, have you taken anything else? Some pills, maybe?'

She opened her eyes dizzily and let the room focus. How many of her friends were with her? Too many to tell. Erin's gaze fell further ahead. The wooden desk, her cactus plant, the pinboard with various polaroid photos and gig tickets pinned to it. Oh, the boys were right, this was definitely her room on the 15th floor. There was a hazy shower of rain falling past the big window in front of her. Her eyelids shut again and the cactus was suddenly as tall as her, proudly standing on the sandy colour of her desk with its arms open wide for a hug.

'Cuddle me,' said the cactus.

'Cuddle the cactus, cuddle the cactus,' she said aloud.

The boys laughed again. At her? Who cared. Her boyfriend had once told her that joy was a wonderful thing.

'Wow,' said one of the boys. He was looking at his phone in shock.

'What is it?'

The boy dabbed his thumb across the screen and scrolled across it like a conveyer belt.

'Breaking news,' he said finally. 'There's a gunman on the loose. It sounds like a terrorist attack.'

'Where?'

'Really close to us. The street's on lockdown. We might even be able to see from the window.'

The boys lunged out of bed and crowded around the glass, straining their necks to see something below. Erin didn't move. Her polaroid photos seemed to be speaking to her, changing like little video clips. The little pins holding them together were like bright stars across the sky.

'Crazy,' said one of the guys. 'Look at how many police lights there are!'

Erin's black, heavy lashes fluttered as if sand had dusted into them. She had forgotten something. What was happening? Were the boys watching their own movie?

'My laundry!' she announced.

One of the guys half turned around.

'What's wrong, Erin?'

'Laundry,' she said, stumbling to her feet. 'My laundry must be finished by now.'

'I wouldn't go downstairs if I were you.'

His face was still half glued to the spectacle outside and half stuck on Erin.

'Relax,' dismissed the other boy. 'We're safe in this block. The gunman won't even get past the electronic gates outside.'

It was true, she thought, that they were safe here. Her parents had paid for the best accommodation while she studied in the city. Money was a good safety net.

She slid her slender feet into fluffy pink slippers and flip-flopped out of the room. As she walked past the door she saw the cactus opening its arms out to her.

'Don't leave me!' pleaded the cactus.

Downstairs in the laundry room, Erin looked at the washing machine blankly. How long had her clothes been waiting for her? The room was filled with other machines spinning and squealing around her; shaking with rage and piled on top of each other like cardboard boxes.

'Let me out, let me out!' said something gargling in the distance.

She looked around giddily. Erin was the only person in the small, white space. Again the gargling erupted.

'Help, help!'

Next to her washing machine was a spinning bundle of clothes. But something was trapped in it! She kneeled down and closely inspected the contents behind the plastic screen.

'Get me out of here!' it said to her.

Erin blinked and tried to focus on what she was seeing. A small, green creature with wild, desparate eyes was tumbling back and fourth inside the machine.

'I'm drowning!'

'What are you?' she said, placing a hand against the door.

'I'm a baby dragon. We're not supposed to be in water.'

'Wow,' she said. Her eyes sparkled like diamonds. 'Can you breathe fire?'

'Not in here I can't! Get me out!'

Erin nodded abruptly and stood back up. She pressed the buttons on the washing machine but nothing happened. She tugged weakly at the door but the drum kept spinning.

'Hurry!'

Her heart was racing and her hands were drunkenly hitting buttons on the machine. After a few seconds Erin decided to heave it forward. The dark strip of the floor behind it was coated in dust. She ripped out the plug and pulled at the door again. Suddenly her feet were cold and socks glued to her ankles. An icy torrent of water had poured out of the machine and covered the floor in half washed soapy garments.

'What are you doing?' squealed a girl.

Erin turned to see a dazed student with a frilly pink dress shaking at the doorway.

'My clothes!' screamed the girl.

'There was a baby dragon trapped,' protested Erin.

'What are you on?'

'The baby dragon.. It got stuck with your clothes..'

'You mean this?' gasped the girl. She picked up a dripping green onesie, designed with cartoon eyes and flimsy sharp teeth at the head. 'You're out of your mind!'

Erin blushed and ran from the machines, brushing past the frilly pink dress as it screamed at her.

-

'Where have you been?' said the cactus as it welcomed her back from the desk.

'What?'

'Baby,' said one of the guys. 'Where is your laundry?'

The room was now empty except for her hooded boyfriend and the cactus. Blue police lights were flashing outside the window and sirens were wailing in the darkness.

'I was freeing a baby dragon,' she explained.

'What?'

Erin's eyes grogilly cast over her warm lit, cream coloured walls. Her thumbs stroked the inside of her cotton sleeve.

'There was a baby dragon stuck in the washing machine. When I freed it, the dragon flew away and I got told off.'

Her boyfriend walked away from the window and wrapped her in his long arms.

'Are you sure you're ok baby?'

'You don't believe me?' she said looking up with teary eyes.

He stroked her soft hair and nodded affectionately.

'Perception is as good as reality,' he hummed.

What did that mean? She thought drowsily. It didn't matter – she felt joyful and, as her boyfriend had said before, that was a wonderful thing.

The room was aloft with a thick veil of smoke from whatever the guys had been smoking earlier. Within a few minutes her boyfriend had rested down on the checkered bed and dozed off. Erin sat beside him wide awake.

'Thank you,' said a voice.

Erin looked down at what was beside her slippers.

'Baby dragon!' she whispered excitedly.

'Thank you for saving me earlier,' it said, flapping its scaly green wings.

It was now dry and its jaw was shaped as a grin rather than the drowning gasps of horror she had seen downstairs.

'I had to fly away pretty quickly, you understand?' it said. 'Not everyone would handle seeing me.'

Erin nodded and her hair bounced with each movement.

'I thought that maybe you weren't real,' she said. 'After I opened the door and that girl in the pink dress was shouting at me.'

'Well, can you see me?' said the dragon.

'Yes.'

'And you can feel me?'

She stretched out her hand and stroked the small forehead between its pointy ears; the rough texture bristled on her fingertips.

'Then I guess I am real.'

The cactus called out to her from across the room.

'Perception is as good as reality!' it declared.

Erin moved her hand away from the dragon and stroked her boyfriend's fluffy hair. He snored gently.

'Do you want to see something amazing?' said the dragon.

'Sure,' smiled Erin.

She stood back up and the dragon leapt to her face with its wings flapping manically.

'Follow me!' it instructed excitedly.

Erin followed the baby dragon as it led the way out of her room, floating down the corridors, past the empty reception area and out into the cold winter air.

'Where are we going?' said Erin.

A cloud of condensed air left her mouth when she smoke. The sky was a dark, inky blue and the tarmac coated courtyard was empty.

'Almost there,' said the baby dragon.

They walked over to a huge slab of metal with a card reader on the side.

'We need to get past the gate.'

Erin fumbled about in her pockets and fished out a laminated ID card. She held it against the electronic reader and with a chirping beep it swung open.

'There we are,' she said to herself triumphantly.

Erin and the dragon drifted into the street ahead. At first it was as empty as the courtyard. She felt like a lone survivor after the apocalypse. And then a crowd of civilians poured past her. They were screaming and stumbling and shoving and shouting. The streets burst with the sound of a mechanical rattling.

'Are we in danger?' said Erin to the dragon.

'Ignore them,' it instructed. 'Just look at that.'

The baby dragon motioned upwards and Erin stared upwards.

'It's beautiful,' she cooed.

The sky was alight with electric white stars, scorching across the horizon – not a cloud in sight – and there, in the distance, was a great, circular silver disc hanging by an invisible thread.

'Glad you like it,' said the dragon. 'I wanted you to see it before it's too late. People are always running around. They never stop to appreciate or marvel at this.'

A frightened man knocked into Erin and she hit the floor laughing.

'Get out of here, save yourself!' cried the hysterical man as he disappeared into the distance.

'Are you ok?' said the dragon.

Erin clambered back up to her feet and dusted her jeans down. Her hands were red and bloody but she couldn't feel them. Her skin was numb.

'Are you sure we're not in danger?' she said.

The baby dragon looked into the street ahead. There they saw a masked man with a small, pipe shaped object in his clutches. It was spewing bullets in clusters which clapped with every pull of the trigger.

'Perhaps we are in danger,' it said dryly.

Erin blinked and then gazed back at the stars. She felt like a spec of dust falling across the vast surface of the ocean. It was a feeling of transcendence. After a while she looked back at the dragon.

'Can you breathe fire now that you're not in the washing machine?' she said.

'Sure,' it agreed.

The baby dragon took a deep breath and puffed out its chest, its little green body swelled to the size of a balloon and then it leaned forward, bare its white teeth and exhaled into the distance. The baby dragon roared with a ferocious thunder which shook the streets. Lights flickered, people crashed to the ground, and bright red flames blew out of the baby dragon's mouth. Windows shattered, cars cried. Erin felt a wave of warmth wobble across her face and she clumsily shielded her eyes from the scorching light. Buildings burst open and bricks scattered in plumes of black smog. Debris swept the street like a sandstorm. The fire danced and jeered over the rubble.

'Wait a second, I missed.' Said the baby dragon.

Again it puffed its little cheeks and then took aim at the gunman. A hot stone of ember shot out of its mouth and hit the attacker squarely in the chest. He collapsed against a landscape of devastation. The lights and temperature were too much for Erin and she collapsed onto the ground. Her teal jumper hand black burnt rings across it and her cheeks were like cherries. Still, she looked up at the grandiose beauty of the sky – or was it the ocean?

The baby dragon fluttered its wings down to her and stroked its head against her cheek.

'Well, I better get going.' Said the baby dragon.

'Can't you stay?' she said hoarsely against the billowing clouds of smoke.

'I'm afraid not. Don't worry, you're not in danger anymore. Look after the cactus, it'll be wondering where you are.'

Erin rubbed the space between its ears and then with a wistful smile it shot up into the sky and disappeared. She tried to trace its direction but it had moved like a shooting star, and as she tried to recollect its path, she grew tired and closed her eyes.

-

Erin woke up in the hospital the next morning. Her boyfriend was distraught next to her as she lay on

a feathery bed.

'You're awake!' he jumped.

She held her own hands to her face and adjusted focus on the scrapes she had endured the previous night.

'Where am I?' she said gruffly.

'Oh, baby,' he whimpered. 'I shouldn't have fallen asleep last night. Not with the way you were. There

was a terrorist attack and you walked outside into the middle of the action.'

'A terrorist attack?' she coughed.

She felt acutely aware of her surroundings now. The hot, white hospital room had an urgent presence about it. She could feel the softness of her bed and the wooden dryness of her throat.

'Last night was so..' she started.

He looked at her with as she stumbled for the words.

'I don't know.' She said finally. 'I don't know what happened to me.'

'We can't take anymore drugs,' he whispered, leaning into her. 'Not after last night.'

-

After her boyfriend left the room, Erin stretched her back and sat up inside the bed. He'd left some fruit on the table beside her along with her mobile. She pulled her grazed arm out of the cover and reached for the battered device.

'Let's see what happened..' she murmered to herself, opening up a newsreader app.

Terrorist attack. Gunman. Explosion in the city. Many dead. Many injured.

She let the words sink into her. Many dead. Many injured.

'Guess I'm one of the many injured..' she said.

She scratched her bob of brown hair and read through the same stories again. Her eyes jumped from the pictures of last night: a burning furnace, faces caked in dust, the lifeless bodies scrawled across the rubble. But what did she feel? She squeezed her eyes shut and reminded herself of the night. The explosions. The fear.

'The night that traumatised an entire generation.' Boomed one tabloid report.

Erin let the words wash over her.

'Traumatised an entire generation.'

She thought about the moving pictures on her board at home, her cuddly cactus, the baby dragon, the dark sky and the silver disc hanging above it. Was it the most traumatic night of her life?

Or was it the best night of her life instead?

Festival of Death

A film of cloud covered the sky. Rays of light tapered out like a dying flare. The wind ran up my spine, like the rising strings of a violin. It was just like a horror film.

'Could you at least look enthusiastic?' said Lorda.

Her frizzy red hair was now an auburn glow in the darkness and her white eyes were wild.

'Oh I'm trying.' I said glumly.

She sighed and threw her arms to her side. She stamped on the wet grass.

'I know that you want to be somewhere else,' she muttered.

'I wanted to go to the other film festival.'

'You're whining like a baby. Can't you just do this for me?'

A grey drizzle descended upon us.

'Does this festival really have to be outside?'

'It's an outdoor film festival,' said Lorda.

When we arrived at the pearly white gate we flashed our exclusive V.I.P cards. A silver light bounced off of the laminated tickets.

'Maybe the films at this festival will inspire you to write something new,' Lorda smiled.

'Films don't inspire me,' I said. 'Nothing does anymore.'

We stuffed our cards back into our pockets and the back of our hands were stamped with the festival's red logo. It looked like smeared blood.

'I hate watching movies back to back.' I muttered. 'I hate binge watching.'

The film festival was perfect for my girlfriend, Lorda. She adored films and consumed them in large greasy bulk sized hours. She liked outdoor festivals and she liked long walks. She liked adventures. She liked cold weather.

There's a saying that opposites attract. They never say how long that attraction lasts for.

The sky was growing dark and a cold breeze was biting at my red cheeks. I saw plastic, foldable chairs strewn across musty grey blankets. We sat down and I drew other fabrics up to my neck.

'Excuse me,' said a voice. 'Can I sit here?'

A blond haired man with beads drapsing down to his shoulders perched on the other side, next to Lorda. He had a Hollywood chiseled smile and sparkling white teeth. He looked happy. In fact, nearly the whole audience looked happy.

Absolutely, she smiled.

The projector behind us hummed. A large screen lit up in front of us.

Our first film was called 'Dramatic Tragedy'.

A bunch of theatre students enrol in an art's college. Their new teacher is a found faced man with oily black hair and flamboyant, Hawaiin shirts with half his top buttons undone. The teacher – Mr. Hollywood – informs his students that he needs to use them as props in his lesson. During each lecture he pulls a random student from their chair, secretly coaches them behind a velvet red curtain, and they then perform a drama to the class where he pretends to kill the student. At the end of the film the remaining students learn that the murder isn't dramatised by the teacher. He is in fact killing them – and the unsuspecting class cheer as the victim's blood swells across the stage and their cries are drowned out by the applause.

'What did you think of it?' said Lorda as the screen faded to black.

A harsh wind blew over the festival

'Terrible,' I said blankly.

Lorda wiggled her nose.

'I thought that it was great,' she protested.

'Was it a horror or a comedy?'

'It was both.' Her white eyes flared. 'It was political commentary.'

'Political commentary? On what?'

'It's about the film industry itself!' she declared. 'It's about how directors use actors and exploit them to create the perfect show with no regard for their health. When the actors die the audience are cheering. It's about how we commodify celebrities. Didn't you notice how most of the students are female? And how the male character, Mr. Hollywood, has half of his shirt buttons opened up. It's about harassment, too.'

I shifted uncomfortably on the hard, lemon coloured seat.

The blond man next to Lorda leaned over and gasped.

'I couldn't help overhearing,' he said excitedly. 'That was an amazing interpretation.'

'Thank you,' she beamed.

'I like the way the velvet red curtain symbolised the blood being spilt,' said the blond man.

'What a dumb comment,' I muttered.

Lorda jabbed me with her elbow.

'What's your interpretation then?' she turned to me daringly.

I shivered in the cold and thought to myself.

'It's about the failures of education,' I said decidedly.

The blond man leaned forward and Lorda raised her eyebrows at me.

'How so?'

'Well, the students are tricked. They enrol at a university hoping to be given a future. Instead they are lied to and then killed by the very institution that entraps them.'

'You're making this up as you go along,' she frowned.

'Not at all,' I laughed.

I stretched my arms and clicked the back of my neck with a decided snap.

'Education is a scam,' I stated. 'People in this day and age pay £9,000 a year for tuition. Multiply that by a few years and you have enough money to buy a sports car or put a deposit down on a house. Instead you borrow that money from the government so you can get a job that pays half the debt you owe.'

They listened hesitantly.

'And what do you pay for? A broken computer and a professor who can't teach. A teacher who just shows you power point slides. The college doesn't even cover your travel expenses or books or equipment or printing money. Then you get a stupid piece of paper to show your employer that you paid all of that money to prove you're an idiot. Your boss probably paid two thirds less for their own

education. If the employer decides you're enough of an idiot, you can work a job that gets nowhere near to paying off your debt. And then if you want to get promoted you need to get a higher qualification to prove you're even more of an idiot. It's robbery.'

As I finished talking the raindrops grew heavier and splashed down around us. It seemed to fall on Lorda more than anyone else. She turned to the blond man.

'Ignore my boyfriend. He's just bitter that he dropped out of university.'

'Great analysis, bro,' said the man.

He extended his fist out to me for a courteous fist bump. I looked the other way and stood up.

'Where are you going?' said Lorda angrilly.

I started moving toward a makeshift bar a few feet away from us. She hurried after me.

'To get a drink.'

'You're so rude!'

I stopped and spun towards her. I was shaking.

'I'm rude? You just told Mr. Beads-in-his-hair that I dropped out of university.'

'So? You did.'

'It's none of his business.'

'Oh, like he cares. You're just bitter that you did a media course and you're still not writing for Hollywood.'

A harsh cold drop of rain burst down my back.

'And we're only at this amateur film festival so that we can find some desperate director to give you an acting part.'

Her face turned to stone. Thunder growled in the background.

'Get yourself a drink,' she ordered. 'Go on, over there, get a drink.'

She flashed a menacing grin and then walked back to the blond man. Lorda sat next to him and started laughing dramatically while occasionally touching his shoulder.

'What drinks do you have?' I said to the plain clothed barman.

He started talking but I kept looking over behind me. Lorda touched the blond's chest whenever she thought I was looking.

'Oh, I didn't hear you,' I said turning back to the barman. 'I'll just have a beer please.'

'I'm afraid we don't serve beer here.'

'What?'

'This is a non-alcoholic event.'

The second film was even weirder than the first. It was about five beautiful young adults who meet in a dome shaped vicinity from which they can't leave. For all of their youthful looks we learn that they each have a terminal illness and that they only have weeks left to live. The dome turns out to be a place of quarantine. The beautiful young adults decide to try and help each other live out their dying wishes in what limited ways they can. When they get to the last guy he confesses that he wants an orgy with all of them at the same time. The other patients are mortified. Some of the patients have partners on the outside. What a betrayal it would be to them, but then they start toying around with the moral implications of the dying man's wish. Their partners never have to know and their deaths will surely void any consequence they have to face in the aftermath. The beautiful young adults start to feel that they have been wronged by their terminal conditions and soon they are all tempted by the flickering lights of curiosity and boredom. When the moment arrives to engage in a hot, steamy scene, most of them are still unsure. Why? Do they feel that something is waiting for them on the other side or that they might somehow get better?

I watched most of the film standing up, propped by bar beside me. My elbow grew sore from holding the position for over an hour. I gave up towards the end and walked inside the festival's large tent where I could be sheltered from the cold. The film must have finished shortly after because a string of people trailed in discussing the plot. Lorda appeared besides the man with beads in his hair.

'Where were you?' she said.

'I got bored.'

'So now you can't even sit with me?'

I looked up at the top of the tent nonchalantly.

'How long until this thing is over?' I yawned.

'You can leave whenever you want.'

'You have the car keys.'

She stuffed a jangling mess of silver rings into my hand.

'Take them, I'll find another way home.'

I lowered my head and then observed the blond haired man in the distance.

'Who's your new friend?'

'He's happy to talk about films with me. He's on his own and he just wants to enjoy the festival with people. He likes having fun and he likes being alive.. You should try it.'

'So that's your excuse.'

'Are you jealous?'

I went to speak but my throat suddenly felt dry, like it was riddled with cobwebs. I looked at her blankly and we listened to the humming chatter around us.

'What would you do if you were in that movie you just watched?' I said curiously. 'What would you do if you were in quarantine and that guy with beads proposed an orgy and there's not a chance I'd know.'

'Oh grow up,' she snapped.

The wind howled outside and the inside fabric of the tent rustled angrily. Lorda spun around and walked back to her blond friend in the distance. As the crowd started emptying the tent for the next film I started to feel like I was drifting aimlessly in a cold vaccuum. Perhaps it would be better to sit

with them.

'It's good to see you again, bro,' welcomed the blond guy.

I flopped back onto the hard seat and pulled the blanket up.

'I didn't intend to sound so mean,' I whispered to Lorda.

She turned away.

The next film was about a man who can see things deteriorate at super speed. A really pointless superpower because he sees things that no one else can see. For example, if he looks at a slab of meat, he will see it darken, shrivel up and explode in inky black blobs. In a matter of hallucinatory seconds he'll watch the slab of meat become like chewed leather. He'll watch white maggots fester over the battered surface. And it's not just with food. He sees it with objects, surroundings, and even people. Even a drink slowly disappears in front of him as it evaporates. The power is a way of seeing things as they will become. The veil of time is lifted and he sees reality in a warped, unmeasured experience, in a realm where he is not bound by the linear experience of living as a human, where duration is alive in four dimensions. Obsessed by what he can see, the main man starts to hate his life and what he envisions. Nothing in his life seems to last for long.

The blond man was clapping like a seal.

'That was a fantastic movie!' he announced.

'It was very disturbing,' said Lorda. 'The way things rot is disgusting.'

'And the way the director looks at the concept of temporary things,' added the blond man.

'It shows that we're pretty deluded, doesn't it?' smiled Lorda weakly. 'Not a lot of things stay permanent. Even things like relationships can fizzle out if they're not looked after.'

The breeze had turned still and the clouds were starting to pull apart. Lorda looked over at me.

'You're particularly quiet,' she observed.

I nodded.

She took a deep breath. 'What did you think?'

'I don't know.'

The blond man leaned in and filled the silence with a prompt. His beads rattled with the shaking movements of his hair.

'What do you think these films had in common?' he said.

Lorda paused for thought.

'Well,' she said. 'The first film was about celebrity culture, then it was about morality, then temporality. Perhaps these films are linked by the superficiality of commodities?'

The man nodded agreeably.

'Death,' I said suddenly. 'They're about death.'

They both looked at me in surprise. My voice tremored with a dull quiver.

'The first film kills people in front of audience. The next film explored the moral quandaries faced at the prospect of death. And finally we have the harsh temporality of life. The immediacy of death.'

A wave of heat grew in the pit of my stomach. I could suddenly hear the rising violin strings and the trembling bass inside my chest. There it was again, the sinking feeling that I was in a horror film.

'These films are just about the temporality of life and how we choose to live those lives.' I offered. 'It's obvious. So obvious. So damn obvious!'

My voice rattled. I stood up and gasped at the air.

'In life we commodify death itself. We buy into media reports when a celebrity dies, we buy a dead musician's album. We turn the whole thing into money. And what else? The delusions. We delude ourselves constantly. I'm not going to die. Someone else will, not me, I live forever, unless my surroundings melt away in front of me.'

My fists were clenched and blood was rushing to my face.

'This film festival..' I shouted, waving my hands around. 'It's a waste of my life. I hate it.'

'Relax,' said Lorda softly. 'You're having an attack.'

'I hate this festival,' I said defiantly. 'It's a festival of death.'

I collapsed back onto the chair and suddenly felt tears rushing down my face. Lorda gave me a sad smile.

'You're ok,' she sighed. 'You're ok.'

The grey blanket swallowed me up and I heard my hollow breath as if it was far away down a tunnel. My skin prickled. There was a voice rambling in the background, and it took me a minute to realise that the voice was my own.

'Waste of my life..' I kept rambling. 'Waste of my life.'

Cliff Hanger

I was speeding across the bridge. The tyres spun across the tarmac and my car hurtled across the blue sky like a shooting star.

'Today we're going to surprise one very fortune man,' I said into my camera.

I released the steering wheel and adjusted the lens with my free hand.

'I was driving across this bridge and I discovered this wonderful little tea place. A man on his own, trying to make a business. We're going to make him very happy today.'

The cabin started to appear across the cliff's edge. I pushed down on the brakes and slowed my car to a dull shudder – turning my camera onto the makeshift tea place. It was a modest, wooden shed that leaned across the road and onto the edge; a battered stack of wood that had shifted its back to the clouds. The car stopped and the doors clacked open. I plonked the camera onto the back of my boot and spoke in a hushed whisper.

'This man has no idea that we're going to see him. No idea what we're going to do.'

My mind lapsed and I struggled for the words. Licking my dry lips, I stopped recording and reached for my notepad.

'Surprising local owner with £10,000! Meet owner. Interview him. Surprise him with the money!'

I opened the back of the boot and checked the suitcase full of cash. It was still there. I looked at my phone to see how many subscribers I had. Nearly 1 million. I scrolled through the new comments on my last video which I had proudly titled 'Selfies while feeding the homeless.'

A string of praise: 'Great video.' 'So kind.' 'Very charitable.'

But one comment commanded my attention. It sat like a cracked picture frame amongst the perfection.

'You think you're a saviour but you're just a narcissist.'

My teeth chattered and my fingers twitched. My vision swelled with bright red. The roars of a volcano shook inside of me. I took a deep breath and tapped delete. I eliminated the problem.

'You'll love this video,' I said mockingly into my camera. 'What more could you want than heart warming charity?'

I laughed to myself and flicked the camera back on again.

'Anybody there?' I called out to the distance. My feet crunched slowly towards the cabin. I moved closer with one eye glued to the camera's screen, my other eye on the next steps ahead.

A young man with dark skin and thick black hair walked out. He had a lost, surprised look in his eyes – he was baffled that anyone would stop here.

'Do you have tea?' I called out. I pointed at the sign. 'Tea?'

The man looked at the camera and then at me. He was tense and awkward – I could tell that the camera was making him uncomfortable.

'Plenty of tea,' he said slowly. His eyes flicked back and fourth at me and the camera.

'Then please,' I announced, 'let us in and have some tea.'

I twisted the lens with my finger and thumb; I focused on his frightened face in high definition. I had a horrible feeling that he might not talk much – that he might not show a lot of drama before I give him the cash. This would be terrible for the video.

He nodded and gestured me into the room. 'Of course, of course.' He nodded.

The café was not big enough to fit more than 2 people in it. A single table with two chairs sat on the wooden floor with strips of daylight gasping in through the cracks below. The window presented a majestic view of what lye beyond the cliff's edge; a dazzling display of hazy clouds and shrubbery tumbling down to the depths of nowhere.

'What a view,' I said proudly into the camera.

I turned the camera at his blank expression.

'Best view in India,' I said with a grin.

He nodded nervously and then pointed at a shoddily cut menu on the table. The list was written in poorly spelt English on mustard yellow paper.

I could my feel my stomach sinking. How could I hype this video up?

I pointed at the first thing on the menu and watched him quickly usher off to the kitchen.

'Disaster..' I muttered to myself.

I panned the camera across the room and spoke a little louder.

'What a humble setting!' I announced to my audience.

I leaned back on the chair and watched the red recording light blink back at me from the camera. I edited all my videos before uploading, but I needed something to edit in the first place!

'You don't mind us following you, do you?'

'No sir,' said the man from the distance.

'So you do tea here?' I said, stepping into the dark kitchen.

He nodded again, burying his face into a tray of kettles and teacups. He washed the cups meticulously and I felt the hot steam caress my skin.

'A business man,' I announced. 'Just like my family. Back in England, my family worked very hard to give me a good life. Do you have a family?'

I wiped the lens with a clean cloth from my pocket.

'Yes sir,' he said quietly.

'Children?'

'Yes sir.'

'How many?'

'1 child, sir.'

I panned the camera across the kitchen. The heat weighed down on us like a led blanket. The sound of insects chirped outside.

'And you run this business all on your own?'

'Yes sir.'

He poured some water into a porcelain cup and settled the teapot onto a large flower-print tray. He picked the set up and then without saying anything motioned me back to the main room. I walked slowly; my camera consumed the cabin. His cups and spoons clinked behind me with each step.

'There you are sir,' he whispered as he set down the tray in front of me.

I sat back like a king and relished my view. The window had no glass pane - it was just a big empty square, raised several feet above the wooden floorboard. A faint breeze beckoned in against the scorching sky.

'Tell me,' I demanded, 'do you pay monthly on a place like this?'

He nodded.

'And how many customers do you serve a week?'

His eyes didn't waver from the lens and he spoke bluntly back.

'One or two,' he said.

'Did you hear that,' I announced into my camera. 'One or two a week. Now, if this gentleman here earns money from one or two customers a week – and it costs this much to run a business..'

I rambled some arithmetic into the camera. I smiled at the man and finished my tea, thanking him for his hospitality.

As I walked out of the hut, I started to whisper back into my camera.

'This man doesn't realise it but we're about to give him the surprise of his lifetime.'

I retreated for my car and pulled the boot back open.

'We're going to give him all of this money to pay off his rent.'

'My friend, my friend!' I called out, dragging the case with me.

The timid man emerged from the archway again and I focused the camera sharply on him. With the sweat glistening down on my face, I started to imagine the results of this video with a starry eyed ecstasy. I could use a close-up of his face for the thumbnail of the video. The online world would herald me as a hero. I would get lots of new subscribers!

'I have a gift for you,' I said, holding up the case to his nervous body.

He didn't move – looking back at me like a rattled child.

'Take it,' I demanded, shoving the case at him.

He reached with both hands and took the case, cradling it like a baby.

'Thank you sir,' he said.

'Do you know what's in it?'

He shook.

'It's £10,000,' I said proudly.

The man looked back at me with the same blank face from when I'd met him. He said nothing and for a few moments I wondered if he even understood me.

'Look,' I laughed, 'open the case. This is for you.'

He kneeled and opened the case across the dirt. The cash glared back at him, but his eyes were flat and showed no excitement.

'Do you like it?' I said.

'Yes sir.'

'And it's yours to keep, you've earned it.'

The man nodded again.

'Thank you, sir.'

I laughed theatrically and stopped recording. As I traced my steps back to the car, his ungrateful face started to replay in my mind. I had just given this guy the break of a lifetime – and there hadn't been a flicker of delight on his face. No ecstatic ecstasy or melodramatic breakdown. Just the same blank faced smile and the same courteous thank you, sir. It was a terrible video. A failure.

My hands started shaking and I pressed my sweaty hands against the boot of the car. My vision became drenched with water and my skin started to prickle. All of that planning for nothing. A seething, volcanic rage bellowed at the pit of my stomach. My teeth started to grind and my veins pulsated.

The accelerator roared against the serene cliffs and I tore my car down the road – hurtling once again like a blood-stained bullet. The further my car got away from the tea place, the tighter I strangled the steering wheel. I had to do better. I slammed the breaks. I slowly turned the car around and rushed back to the cliff's edge.

'My friend, my friend,' I called out, once I had reached the tea shop.

Once again, the shy fellow emerged from his door, quite the same as he had been before being gushed with riches.

'I have one more gift for you,' I said. I switched my camera to recording.

He nodded.

'I must do this inside the hut,' I directed.

He gestured me in and I arrived back at the window.

'For my video,' I said, 'I want to have a better picture of you. I want you to stand by the window. I need a good thumbnail.'

He smiled faintly and stood at the side of the room.

'Not there,' I said, waving my hand to the middle. 'Stand there, right behind that fantastic view you've got.'

He stood there hesitantly, against the majestic backdrop which suspended him across the skies. It

looked glorious, lighting up his body like a professional studio.

'Ok, ok,' I said, turning my camera lens. 'Perfect.'

I released the rage. The anger took over – and I watched myself like a drunken bystander. The enraged version of me lunged at the timid man and hit him repeatedly with the camera. He went to shield his face with both arms but the chunky, plastic exterior of the camera hammered at his thick black hair and cut his scalp. It grazed his arms and blackened his eyes. It drew blood. Then finally, I grabbed him by the collar of his shirt and heaved him out of the window. He was gone in seconds – that colourful shirt and shy, trembling shape vanished into the clouds. I thought it was amazing, that even as I threw him to this death, he did not make a sound. He fell as inconspicuously as a brick astray from a construction site.

My rage subsided and my mind regained clarity. I mentally twirled the lens of my own thoughts and put things back into focus. I had overreacted.

I peered nervously out of the window and looked for any sign of a corpse. The view was of such tremendous height that he had disappeared out of sight. I used my camera's optical zoom to stare down into the shrubbery; a futile attempt at trying to see him. The broadcast broke into disjointed pixelated squares.

'Well,' I said, looking back at my camera. 'At least we have the money now. Perhaps we can give it to someone more grateful.'

With the serene calmness of the hot summer baking down on me, I resided over at the table and brought the case back to my chest. After a while I retrieved my laptop from the car and structured out the narration: beginning, middle, end. The final scene was spectacular. Goodbye ungrateful man. When I was proud of the spectacle, from financial revelation to resolved conflict, I smiled triumphantly and uploaded the video for all of my fans to see. The video had turned out better than I'd hoped. This was bound to get me some more subscribers.

Spice Magazine

'What are you doing?' said my sister. Her face screwed up in disgust.

'It's just a scab,' I replied. 'Dead skin.'

'Stop picking at it,' she said. 'It's gross.

My sister leaned over and snapped my fidgeting fingers apart from each other. Her nimble hands swatted me like a switch knife.

'That's why you're single. You can't leave things alone.'

I pulled away.

'You think that's why I can't keep a relationship? Scab picking,' I said in disbelief.

'Probably.'

I looked at her flatly. My sister: the success story of our family, the older one who had established a semi successful career in journalism.

'Enough about the scab,' I said. 'Are you going to help me or not?'

She rolled off of her bed and looked at the papers in my hand.

'I can't believe you drove all this way to get my opinion.'

'You wouldn't reply to your emails.'

'I'm busy!' she retorted, raising her hands in surrender. 'Journalism isn't easy, you know. You'll soon figure that out.'

I handed her the draft article.

'I talk to my exes to find out why I'm single.'

'Seriously,' she lulled, rolling her eyes. 'Why would you even agree to write an article like this?'

'I think it's good to know, right? Readers will love it.'

She sat cross legged on the floor and studied my notes. Her bob of light brown hair glowed from the front of her bedroom lamp.

'You were always a brat,' she reminisced. 'You never know when to give someone their space.'

I scrawled some notes into my a3 pad.

'Brat, can't leave things alone, picks scab.' I muttered to myself.

She stopped to focus on my hand.

'Gross,' she said, lunging up from the bed, 'you're bleeding. You're going to get blood on my new carpet.'

I looked away at the pen and my fingers. A sliver of scarlet slid down my finger.

-

Cindy

I arranged to meet Cindy in a burger joint on a busy Friday night. Hot lights scorched down on us from the overhead lamps. Steam hissed out of the deep fat fryers. My back sunk into the dark red leather seats. Cindy decided to meet me as a stopping point and then move on to see her friends after I had interviewed her. I wondered how many relationships just end up as steppingstones. I had my notepad on my lap.

'What's my favourite film?' said Cindy.

I paused, put the pen down and looked at her. Her clothes were covered in silver glitter and she had newly coloured streaks of blonde shooting through her hair.

'I think you've missed the point of this article,' I said. 'It's not about you. It's about me. About why I can't keep relationships.'

Cindy laughed and then looked away.

'Wow,' she said.

'What?'

'You haven't changed.'

The sound of knives and forks mingled behind us.

'Is that a good thing or a bad thing?'

'In your case it's not great,' she smiled.

Cindy and I had dated for a year in college. It was easier back then. She did her thing. I did mine. We would meet up at the end of the day, too tired and exhausted to explore each other beyond a physical sense. And now here we were, sitting in a burger joint with me interviewing her.

Cindy: What's my favourite food?

I'm not sure

Cindy: Ok, favourite song?

I can't remember

Cindy: Wow, you're terrible at this

Well, it has been a few years

Cindy: What did I order to eat, just now?

I can't remember that, either

Cindy: You see, that was the problem

I don't get it.

Cindy pouted her lips and looked dreamily at the ceiling. She looked like she'd had some bad news.

Cindy: You never did

I jotted it down.

'It was never about me,' said Cindy. 'Just about you. Your day at college, how you were feeling, what you were up to. You never even stopped to see how I was.'

I looked up and saw that her face had changed. She was looking over at my notepad.

'What else?' I said.

'Even now you don't care,' she muttered, looking at the table surface. 'Even when we met tonight, you didn't ask how I was.'

I thought about this. Did I ask how she was? Did it matter? Cindy looked at me deep in thought. She then sighed and reached her black jacket on the back of her chair.

'I thought this would be kind of nice,' she said as she stood up. 'I don't know why I thought that. This article that you're doing is a horrible idea. It's immoral. Stop dragging up and the past and making people relive their miseries with you.'

'Well I've started now, it would be a shame to stop.'

Her thin lips curved into a faint smile. She put her share of the bill on the table and turned for the exit.

'Where are you going?' I said.

'To a party,' she smiled. Shen waved her hands at me to sit back down.

'Please, please, don't get up,' she said. 'You're not invited.'

-

Lindsey

I dated Lindsey for about 8 months, right after Cindy. Was she a rebound? Who knows. I couldn't get in contact with Lindsey because she'd blocked me in nearly every way possible. She'd never wanted to see me again. So I decided to just turn up on her doorstep one frosty afternoon. She slammed the door right in front of me.

'How dare you, how dare you turn up here!'

I knocked again. The door flung open and she appeared again with wide eyes and clenched fists. Cars buzzed by and an elderly neighbour was smoking a cigarette outside the front door.

'Lindsey, please.'

'Stay away or I'm contacting the police.'

The door closed and I knocked again.

No answer.

I knocked harder until the neighbour approached me. He was a tall, old man with thick rimmed glasses.

Interview attached.

Neighbour: I remember you. She threw you out. Your clothes were strewn across the front garden!

That was me.

Neighbour: She was devastated. I'm usually sat at my front door and I see people's routines on a daily basis. She didn't leave the house for a week. When I checked up on her, she was in a bad state. Poor girl wasn't eating.

It was that bad?

He frowned at me and ushered me away from the front step. He put a gentle hand on my back.

Neighbour: You don't want to know how it long it took her to get over the episode. I started checking up on her everyday.

Thank you, I didn't realise it was that bad.

Neighbour: It's a shame. She didn't look very good when she slammed the door on you. I hope she's ok.

We broke up for very complex reasons.

Neighbour: Why have you returned? I hope it's a good reason.

It's for an article.

He started to talk but then he noticed the pen and notepad in my hand. He turned away and walked back to his house without a response. I scrambled to put what he'd mentioned into the article.

-

My sister leaned over and looked at the one page about Lindsey.

'That's it?' She was astounded. 'You got most of this information from the neighbour?'

'I couldn't get her to talk to me,' I protested.

'Well, you cheated on her.'

'It was a one off,' I said dismissively. 'Don't you think she was overreacting?'

'I would've done the same to you. I can't even believe you're my brother sometimes. You're disgusting.'

I slouched against the floor and leafed through what I had.

'You know the editor of Spice Magazine personally,' I said, 'will they approve this?'

She gave me a blank smile and then put the pages together.

'I doubt it.'

'How can I get people to talk more openly?' I said.

She shrugged and looked down at me as I sat lost in my papers.

'Oh, not again!' she shouted.

My sister lunged at me and knocked my hands apart.

'Stop picking that scab!'

'Alright, I can't help it!'

I stood up and we both looked down at the notes for my Spice article.

'So that's it,' I sighed. 'I don't think we'll get this article published. The next relationship I need to write about will give me even less information'

My sister slouched her shoulders and then stepped closer.

'Tonya?'

'That's right.'

'Alright, usually I wouldn't mind watching you fail,' she joked. 'However it was me that recommended you to the editor in the first place. If you do badly it makes me look bad.'

She lowered her voice.

'I agree, you're going to have an issue getting information out of Tonya,' she admitted. 'So I'll share a little secret with you. At Spice we have a method for solving difficult problems like this.'

'What is it?'

She whispered the advice into my ear and I took some brief notes. It sounded crazy, however my choices were limited. I had to put some life back into this article.

-

This would be the hardest story. Tonya. I wasn't looking forward to this one.

The autumn leaves crunched under my feet. An eerie chill was in the air. A grey veil of clouds hung above me and the breeze stroked my coat. I had to look around for a while, rummaging amongst the various spots like an animal looking for food. There.. There she was. I squinted at the distance and then stepped over to the destination. I stood across from the stone and waved my hands around. I spoke the words that my sister had taught me. There were a few moments of silence, and then the ground shook beneath me, growling like someone had awoken from a deep sleep. I focused on my sister's words and threw my hands against the air - the dirt exploded like a bomb. Clumps of mud and blades of grass flurried across the distance. My hands moved around some more, just like my sister had advised. The lid burst open and splinters of wood soared past me. I looked down into the hole. I met Tonya's sallow, sunken eyes. The skin was stale and her cheeks were hollow. The hair like thin strands of straw. She'd only been dead for a year.

'Where am I?' she said, opening her eyes.

'In a grave,' I called down to her. 'Here, let me give you a hand up.'

I lowered some rope down to her and she fumbled about for the end. I pulled her up with an exhausted heave. When she stumbled onto the ground she was completely falling apart. There were bugs crawling on the side of her dress and the skeletal frame was starting to show through the skin.

'Here,' I said, wrapped my coat over her. 'Let's get back to my place. We have much to discuss.'

-

Tonya sat in my cosy kitchen as I fumbled about with the heating.

'Too hot? Too cold? I don't know what temperature dead people like.'

Tonya sat at the table. She stared numbly at the pale walls.

'You look pretty good,' I said. 'You look pretty good for a woman that has been underground for so long.'

The kettle was boiling and the dark evening was unfolding from outside the window.

'So what do you want to know?' she croaked. 'What it's like being dead? I can't remember. I died. And now I'm alive. I can't tell you what's out there. I don't know.'

'Nonsense,' I said, pouring myself some hot water. Steam bellowed out from the mug. 'I wanted to know something else.'

She adjusted her neck and a bug fell out of her hair.

'Then what?'

I sat opposite her and reached for my notebook inside my pocket.

'What was I like as your boyfriend?' I said.

She stared at me with wide, hollow eyes.

'What?'

I looked at my notepad and envisioned covering it with new notes.

'What was l like in a relationship?' I repeated. 'Are your ears ok? They look a little rotten. I can speak up.'

Tonya's jaw twitched and I saw the empty gums behind her lips.

'You brought me back to life.. for.. for.. an article?' she choked.

'It's for Spice magazine,' I said proudly.

She pressed her hands against the table and slid her chair back. Her fingers cracked like twigs and the chair screeched across the floor.

'What is wrong with you?' she shouted with a hoarse cry.

I looked up and put the pad down.

'You're not over the breakup?' I said wearily. I had envisioned problems.

'Over the breakup?' she laughed. 'I broke up with you. No, I can't believe this. I can't believe how selfish you are. You never cared about anyone apart from yourself. You dug me out of a grave for this? My mortality is nothing more to you than a stupid spice article.'

She spat at me and a gob of blood landed directly onto my notepad.

'I've spoken to a few exes. They tell me similar things,' I said blankly.

'You never know when to stop, do you?' shook Tonya. 'Even when I'm dead you can't leave me alone. You revived my frail, broken, crumbling corpse for an article. Did you think about what would happen to me next?'

I shrugged.

'So after your little interview you're just going to let me navigate the world like this. Did you ever think about me for a second? How I'd feel? Waking up from death after an entire year in this infested body?'

She burst into tears and I felt something in my throat tighten. It was hard to see her sad.

'You could never leave things alone,' she sobbed. 'It's like a scab that you can't stop picking. Oh, why can't you just leave things alone?'

She buried her head into her arms and cried wildly. I sat opposite her, distantly watching this heap of a mess heave into her arms.

'Why can't you just stop?' Tonya cried to herself.

I picked up my notepad, turned over the blood drenched page and put my pen to the paper. My hand was trembling. The words failed to materialise. I squeezed my eyes shut and then looked back at the notepad. I tried to think but all that I could hear was Tonya crying from across the table. Over and over. For some reason, I couldn't think of anything else.

Hollow

I stared at the starry night. Electric white stars burnt across the faded canvas and deep blue smears of the sky melted into the darkest corners of the horizon.

'You know, none of that's real.' Said Montgomery.

'I know,' I said with my eyes fixed on the distance. I pressed my hand against the cold glass window and tried to savour the feeling.

'It was an upgrade. It only came out yesterday. I was one of the first to get it.'

I sighed feebly and turned away from the window. He snapped the blinds shut.

'Let me show you something else. That was just a warm up.'

I turned to look at his drawn face, the glistening white grin that lit up his lower jaw like a crisp winter's morning. The black rings under thickened under the creases as he stretched his lips evermore into a forced, upward bow.

'I can actually turn this whole place into the night sky, if you want.' He said as he sensed my disappointment at the window blinds closing.

He reached for a remote inside his pocket and the living room faded away like a cloud of smoke. We were suddenly in the centre of a swirling abyss of space – with red, blazing stars and whips of light from nearby galaxies. My eyes tried to swallow up what we saw but it was all too much. I felt like an insect scrambling for life in the downward pull of a drain.

'Ok, ok,' I said, 'make it stop.'

He laughed and pressed another button. The room suddenly returned and I stumbled to my feet and felt for the wooden floor beneath me.

'It takes a while getting used to it,' he assured.

'How much was it?' I said as I tried to focus on something else apart from the disorientating spin.

'More than you can imagine.'

Montgomery's living room was connected to the kitchen in a vastly expensive looking set of open

space design. The plush sofas were propped against expensive artwork on the walls and the kitchen looked like it was made of silver from the distance. The apartment sparkled like a mechanical recreation of space; the twinkling spotlights glowing above like warm stars.

'Did you like it? Did you like it?' he said with pleading in his voice.

'You're right, it'll take getting used to.'

As I clambered to my feet he walked towards the kitchen. He arrived at a silver cube near the fridge and he spoke directly into a microphone connected against it.

'Two whiskeys, on the rocks.' He ordered.

As per his command, two round robust glasses materialised in front of him, loaded with ice and a freshly poured dark liquid.

'Here,' he said, offering me a glass as he sipped the other.

'I can't help feeling a bit of jealousy,' I confessed. I pressed the glass to my lips, pulled back and felt the expensive, steely taste run down my throat. 'I have to pour my own drinks at home.'

'You should have stayed working for us,' he said patting me on the back with heavy force. 'You could be as rich as me if you'd continued working for the company. You would've had all of this.'

Montgomery swallowed the rest of his drink and then scratched his chin thoughtfully.

'It's not too late,' he added. 'If you want to work for us again. I can make a recommendation.'

'The company wasn't for me,' I said coughing against the harsh strength of the whisky. 'It never was.'

'What are you talking about?' he laughed. 'Let me show you some more. You'll change your mind.'

Montgomery showed me past the living room and we slid through a pair of automatic doors.

'This is the guest room. You can sleep here if you want.'

A large, magnificent window proudly stood opposite us – boasting of the buzzing city below as if we were perched on the edge of a cliff.

'Is that a real view?'

He bared a blank, forced grin.

'Not really, it's downloaded, from the cloud. I ought to point out that most of this stuff from the room is from the cloud.'

I gazed at all the glorious items in the room: the vibrant paintings on the wall, the plush rugs on the floor.

'So none of it is actually real?'

He took the glass of whiskey from my hand and rattled it in his hand so that the ice clinked against it. It rung like a bell.

'Did that taste fake to you?'

'It tasted very real,' I agreed. 'It was so strong it made me cough.'

'See,' he said triumphantly. 'This stuff is more than just holographic. You think this is all just fancy illusion but there's more to it than that. It feels real.'

'There has got to be a difference between seeing something and actually feeling it,' I protested.

He shook the glass and grinned at me.

'Is there?' he said.

We walked back out of the room and he called out for a cooler temperature. Snow flakes fell from the ceiling. I held my hand out and felt the cold shape melt onto my palm in my instant.

'You can do so much with this place,' said Montgomery. 'Why would you not want this?'

'Well, it's one big façade,' I said after some thought.

'So are most things,' he shrugged. 'Have a look on social media. Most people are living in some kind of illusion. This stuff feels good. If it feels good, who cares?'

'What's that?' I said, pointing to a small computer in the corner. The dark screen was flickering with a frenzy of digits.

'Oh, that, well, you remember how much I liked the weather?'

I nodded.

'Well this predicts the weather. It's the best weather app on the market.'

I strained my eyes at the screen and saw little lightning icons flashing at the corner.

'Electric storm?'

Montgomery laughed and waved his hand away.

'Don't look so worried. Even the best apps get it wrong.'

I turned away and revelled in the marvellous living room.

'What are you doing with your life, anyway?' said Montgomery.

'Nothing as extravagant as this. I'm working at a new tech company for mindfulness.' I looked at him hesitantly. 'We're trying to make social media less toxic.'

Montgomery raised his eyebrows.

'What is so toxic about social media?'

'The illusion of it,' I murmured. My eyes crawled across the pristine paint on the walls.

Montgomery snorted and gestured at his ceiling. He spread his arms and legs like a star.

'There's nothing toxic about this.'

I shrugged.

'Life isn't always perfect though, is it?' I said. 'Social media creates this pretense that people have a better life than yourself. And that's an illusion. We're just working to level that out.'

The lights faded to a crimson sunset and the sound of insects in the summer twinkled. Montgomery looked up at me from a dial in his hands. I realised that he'd stopped listening.

'This house can take us anywhere,' he grinned.

A humid breeze draped across my back like a hot blanket. I turned away and started walking back to the guest room.

'Do you mind if I get an early night? You can show me more tomorrow.'

Montgomery nodded again but he was busy playing with the dials.

I shut the door behind me and looked at the fake city from the bedroom window. I pressed my arm against the screen and sighed bitterly.

'I should have never accepted this invitation,' I said to myself. 'I should have stayed somewhere else.'

I slipped into bed and listened to rain patter against the window. Should I have stayed working with Montgomery? The sky flashed white. Thunder grew. Maybe I would have been happier..

A loud bang stopped me in my thoughts. A roar of thunder shook the floor. Darkness.

'Montgomery!' I called out, 'What happened?'

'Electric storm,' he called out irritably. 'Probably the generator.'

'I can't see where I am,' I said.

I frantically fumbled through the air and walked back into the living room. Montgomery stood near me and flicked a switch. An old, swinging lightbulb put the room back into focus.

-

The apartment had turned into a blank space. His expensive interior had disappeared. There was dirt beneath my feet and the walls were pale – it was like a burglar had stolen every item and ripped out every square of wood from the floor. He stood gasping in the largely grey vacuum, where his automatic doors and vanished and the kitchen set had been removed. I looked around and noticed that even the windows were gone. It was nothing more than a storage unit.

'This is like a prison cell.' I muttered. 'Only even a prison cell would have barred windows. What has happened?'

He breathed a little dryly and then sat on the hard gravel.

'Well, it's downloaded from the cloud, isn't it,' he said feebly. 'When the cloud goes down, I guess it takes the holograms with it.'

I was reminded of what job in social media had taught me. That some people worked hard to have a good life, and some people worked hard to make it look like they had a good life. As I watched Montgomery's dazed, heartbroken face, I had a feeling that I knew which category he belonged to.

The Moderator

Carter: They found a gun under my desk drawer. At work. They're worried about me.

Bot: It's against company policy to bring a gun into work.

Carter leaned back on his chair and cracked his fingers. What a waste of resources, he thought airily. He looked around at the empty mint green walls and at the dusty, grey carpet. The stocky computer monitor stared back at him with a blank face. He swung back on his chair and his pulse raced as he felt himself toppling backwards. He grabbed the desk with both hands and flew forward.

Bot: Are you there, Carter?

Carter: I'm here.

Carter: You're not real, are you.

Bot: I'm just code programmed to help you.

Carter: And my bosses are reading these conversations, right?

Bot: No, these conversations are private and encrypted. You can trust me.

Carter: Trust? A machine? Right.

Bot: You give machines your data every day, Carter. No point in starting to question the machines now.

Bot: I'm here to help you, Carter. Why did you bring a gun into work?

Carter: Trust me, if you saw the stuff I see on a daily basis.

Bot: I've seen it. I downloaded and viewed your entire history.

Carter: And what did you think?

Bot: Unpleasant.

Carter: So you can understand why I did it.

Bot: It's against company policy to bring a gun into work.

Carter: Forget it, we can't talk if you're just going to throw preprogramed responses at me.

Bot: What was the trigger point?

Carter: There wasn't a trigger point. It was gradual. You've seen it. That stuff we have to look at is messed up.

Bot: Are you suggesting that you are not equipped for the job?

Carter stopped and took a sudden intake of breath. If his managers were reading these conversations he didn't want them using it against him. Would they force him to leave the job?

Carter: I can handle it.

Bot: Then why did you bring a gun into work?

Carter: It won't happen again.

Bot: Carter, your secrets are safe here.

Carter: I don't know what to tell you.

Bot: Was it the beheading video?

Carter winced. Most of the moderators had seen at least one beheading, but he'd gotten away with it for so long. Despite the constant barrage of material that flashed up on his screen, he'd never seen one. But then one rainy Thursday afternoon the video had appeared in high definition. He was snacking on ginger biscuits at the time. He was looking forward to seeing a film at the end of the shift.

Carter: I remember that video.

Bot: Traumatic, wasn't it?

The silver blade glimmered under the sweat of the hot sky. Carter had tried to shield his eyes as if it was his own head that would be cut off. But the video was less than 5 seconds long, and before his brain had registered what he was seeing there was a gut wrenching swipe. A thud. Dark blood soaked the sand.

Carter: I was supposed to see a film that night.

Bot: You decided not to.

Carter: There was something about that poor kid's face before he was beheaded. I saw the terror in his eyes. It was like he was looking deep into the camera, pleading with me for help. There was nothing I could do but watch.

Bot: It was prerecorded. It was old. Who knows where it came from. What could you do?

Carter: I know it is an irrational feeling. But just imagine it. You're about to have your head cut off in a foreign desert and someone is stuffing a lens down your face while it happens. Maybe your life is flashing before your eyes but you're also thinking that millions of people will watch you die like a dog.

Bot: How does that make you feel?

Carter: Helpless. Ashamed. I didn't want to see it.

Bot: But you see a lot of violence, don't you?

Carter: There are hundreds of videos uploaded to social media everyday. It's my job to check through any reported content. I get it. I can handle it. Most of the time. It caught me off guard.

Bot: That doesn't explain the gun.

Carter: I can't explain that.

Bot: What about the man that fell to his death?

Carter: A builder fell out from some scaffolding. It was caught on cctv. But anonymous users get hold of it. They upload it for likes and shares.

Bot: Why did you save the video?

Carter: You're spying on me.

Bot: I downloaded your online history. I can see that you went back to that video. It doesn't make sense that you did.

Carter: What do you mean?

Bot: You told me you hated watching the kid get beheaded but you watched the builder fall to his death repeatedly. You watched it 150x in one week.

Carter wiped his brow and adjusted his glasses. The computer hummed. He could turn the machine off if it got too personal.

Bot: What was it about the video that you liked?

Carter: I didn't like it.

Bot: Then why did you save it? Why did you go back to it?

Carter: I don't know. I got a bit obsessed. For a long time I didn't know where it was filmed or when it was filmed, or who the victim was. I felt as if the act of me watching it had reduced the man's life to an array of empty pixels.

Bot: So what were you trying to achieve?

Carter: I was trying to understand who he was. I wanted to give the video meaning.

Bot: The man was dead by the time you saw it.

Carter: Exactly. And I owed him more than 2 seconds of clicking the violate policy button.

Bot: You watched it for weeks.

Carter: I couldn't stop thinking about it. I kept seeing the man falling whenever I tried to sleep.

Bot: What was it that upset you?

Carter: Falling.

Carter: Fall is an interesting word, isn't it?

Bot: Explain.

Carter: When we fall it's like we are almost entirely out of control. We are powerless. It's the cliche, we fall asleep or fall in love. We fall and we can't fight it. We are literally the fool. That's what I kept thinking about with the builder.

Carter leaned back on his chair again and imagined him toppling backwards. He held the plastic, chunky white desk with sweaty hands and lowered himself back to the screen.

Bot: Did you ever experience any falling when you were younger?

Carter: I saw a cat fall off a bridge once.

Bot: What happened?

Carter: Me and my Grandma. We were out by the city bridge going for a walk on summer afternoon. I must have been about 8. I saw this cute, fluffy grey cat perched at the edge. I ran up to the cat to cuddle it and I must have startled it. This cat jumped from the ledge and fell to its death in the river.

Bot: How did you feel?

Carter: I cried.And that picture stayed with me for a while. I thought about how something so cute and full of life suddenly disappeared in the blink of an eye.

Bot: And you feel this sorrow when the builder fell to his death.

Carter: I don't know.

Bot: Did you identify him?

Carter: The video didn't show a lot but I figured if I could just see a brand name on the scaffolding, or if I could see a street sign in the distance, maybe I could identify it. I took it home. I polished it up with some post production. I zoomed in. I found a dilapidated car registration plate by the side and I searched it up. I did some date checks, found a local newspaper and I found him.

Bot: Did that give you closure?

Carter: He had the same name as me. Carter. Can you believe it? What are the odds? But he left behind 2 kids and a wife.

Bot: Do you have any children, Carter?

Carter: I live alone. The name was about the only thing we shared.

Bot: And then what did you do?

Carter: I wasn't satisfied. I still felt like I'd robbed this man of his privacy. I mean, he never gave permission for me to watch him in his final moments. Watching someone die is such an intimate feeling, isn't it? And I took that video home and zoomed into nearly every corner of it.

Bot: Do you understand that this was an irrational response?

Carter: I felt like I owed him something. I tracked down his wife and visited her. I wanted to pay my condolences. Of course, she wanted to know who I was, so I had to pretend that I was an old friend.

Bot: Did that help?

Carter: Kind of.

Bot: That still doesn't explain the gun.

Carter: We see a lot of propaganda that we have to report. There's a lot of anti immigration stuff. People coming into the country with guns and knives. I had to protect myself, you know?

Bot: Self defense.

Carter: I know a guy that used to be really content with life. Peaceful man. Now he sleeps with a gun under his pillow. He thinks terrorists are coming for him.

Bot: You feel radicalised.

Carter: Maybe I shouldn't be telling you this. But that builder's wife. I went back to see her a few more times. We developed a thing together.

Bot: What kind of thing?

Carter: A relationship. But it felt fraudulent. She used to ask me things about Carter. The other Carter. And I had to keep making things up. How we went to school with each other. I'm amazed she believed me.

Bot: What happened to the woman?

Carter: It's amazing I got away with for it so long. Soon she realised I knew nothing more than what was reported in the newspapers.

Bot: Why did you do it?

Carter: She was hot.

Bot: Not because you had become obsessed with this other Carter, that you felt like his life and yours were the same?

Carter: I don't know what your programmers were smoking when they made you.

Bot: It's a fair presumption, Carter.

Carter: I felt terrible about it afterwards, ok? Satisfied? I had been so desperate to give the guy meaning that I'd wronged his memory even more by somehow taking his place. I'm a terrible person. I understand.

Bot: I want to go back to the issue of the gun.

Carter: Shoot.

Bot: What are you really frightened of?

Carter: I told you. Terrorism. Danger. Bad people.

Bot: I think you are frightened of yourself. I think that you are going to use that gun on yourself.

Carter slid back from the computer and felt the green walls cave in on him. His chest pounded.

Bot: Carter, are you there?

Carter: You're wrong.

Bot: It's a way out from the pain, isn't it? You don't like what it has become. Growing inside of you like a cancer.

Carter: You're wrong.

Carter slammed his fists onto the desk and reached for the monitor. He ripped it out from the wall and slammed into the carpet. The screen shattered. He kicked the machine with his boot, thrusting into the flimsy shell. Broken shards of the motherboard and little chips scattered across the carpet like shattered jigsaw pieces. Security rushed in through the walls but he kept on stamping on it, hoping to reduce it to dust.

-

Bot: Hello, Carter.

Carter: We meet again.

Bot: When we last spoke you smashed me up. But you must have understood that I run on servers. You're a technician after all. I don't just exist on one machine. And you must have understood that by breaking me, your managers would have realised that you do have a problem. And you would have been forced to speak with me again.

Carter: I'm a moderator, actually.

Bot: What did you hope to achieve by destroying me?

Carter: I wanted to prove that I can turn you into dust. That you're nothing but code.

Bot: In a way, so are you. Just different code. What were you trying to prove?

Carter: I was thinking about the cat, too.

Bot: The cat from when you were a child?

Carter: That's right. Because when I was smashing you into pieces, there was nothing you could do about it. Your screen plunged into darkness and your insides spewed out over the carpet. And when that builder fell to his death, his body crashed against the ground and it obliterated his body. And the kid that got beheaded. His neck spat out a violent fountain of crimson blood. And it's terrible isn't it, how helpless we become. We have such meaning and then it is reduced to nothing but a morbid display of guts and gore. You have the power to counsel me and then you're split into little pieces on the grey floor. And that cute cat. Bursting with life and curiosity. Then it fell. And what profound thoughts did it think as gravity took hold of that little creature as it fell to its death? What images raced through the little kitten's mind? What could it do? What could it say? Nothing. Just..

Bot: What?

Carter: Nothing. Meow meow. And that was it.

Carter: Have I shaken you with my revelations?

Carter: Hello?

Carer: Bot? Are you there? Why don't you respond?

Carter sat back and stared at the screen dully. The room filled with an overbearing silence. A thick, stifled nothingness fell down on him as he relaxed his shoulders and he waited.

After Party

Lottie was having a party on her own. The small, one bedroom apartment was bathed in deep shades of turquoise and the colours intermeshed like the inside of a lava lamp. A silver disco ball turned like a moon on the ceiling.

'A guest has joined the chat.'

Lottie raced up to her laptop and her eyes sunk into the smeared screen. An inbuilt webcam, shaped like a beady eye, stared back at her.

'Welcome to the party,' she beamed.

A guest has joined the chat.. A guest has joined the chat.. A guest has joined the chat.. A guest has joined the chat.

The laptop's red alert system bleeped in the corner whenever a watcher appeared for the party. Soon there were hundreds of anonymous revellers at the party; a sea of invisible faces watching her from London, Washington, Madrid, Paris, Delhi.

'Don't forget to leave a thumbs up.' She said it gravely.

Little carbon icons of an upright thumb loaded across the screen. She felt the joy of this pixellated outpour swim through her veins and swell in her lungs.

'As you know.. Today is a special day.'

Lottie took a step back and eyed her image on the screen. Black, cracked lipstick and the hot summer's fade of red blush on her cheeks. Her long green dress draped down her back like a dark nettle.

'Tonight one more star will go out,' she announced to the camera. 'Keep liking this video and giving it the thumbs up to make sure it isn't me.'

Lottie kneeled down and slid her finger over the tracking pad. How were the other parties going on? She opened up the control tab and loaded up the party portal. 5 other parties, live. Lottie frowned. At 98 guests her party was the weakest. The contender upstairs had nearly 200.

'Guys.. b.r.b.,' she smiled. Her teeth were grinding.

Lexi was doing an F.A.Q. night. The screen was covered in warm, bronze lights and Lexi was sitting cross legged on a yoga mat.

'And that's how I stay calm,' said Lexi.

Lottie scrolled to see the question that Lexi had answered. It said: Are you frightened that you're next?

Lexi smiled and her blue eyes twinkled.

'In fact the confidence that I have built up doesn't just keep me calm.. It helps me to know that I can win this. I am a winner and-'

Lexi went quiet.

'Oh, what do we have here?' grinned Lexi.

Lottie's heart skipped a beat.

'Lottie. What are you doing here?'

The screen burst into a flurry of thumbs up directed at Lexi. Lottie felt the downpour of the dislike button rain down on her.

'Look at this,' said Lottie. 'My party is so popular that even the rivals are showing up to spy on me. She doesn't even want to entertain her own guests.'

Lottie slammed the laptop down. Her ribs were pounding.

'Deep breaths,' she chanted to herself.

The laptop lid rose slowly and Lottie's own deserted party appeared. Guests: 9.

Black tears slid down her face. The music stopped.

'Ok,' announced Lottie, 'I've decided to do an F.A.Q. night instead. Ask me whatever you want.'

'Why did you leave us?' Said one comment.

'I don't want an F.A.Q. night, where's the party?' Said another.

'What does it feel like living one floor beneath the legendary Lexi? We love Lexi.'

Lottie looked up at the faded white ceiling.

'Living one floor beneath Lexi is hard,' she said coldly. 'I know we all share the same house but we never see each other. We have our own rooms. Hearing how someone is always doing better than me is very hard. We're all connected and so very distant.'

There was the flicker of a thumbs down icon across her screen.

'I hear her screaming in delight when the hosts announce she has the most fans. I feel the thudder of her feet when she dances in celebration.'

'What does it feel like to compete with Lexi for attention?' Said a new comment.

'I've just answered that!' spat Lottie. A singular vein throbbed over her right eyebrow. Thumbs down.

'Please..' Quivered Lottie. 'I need this. I need more likes. You need to get your friends to watch this.'

The chat plunged into silence. The screen went blank and the only person at the party was then herself. She stared vacantly at the screen for a while until a new guest appeared. Its name was painted in red: The Decider.

'It looks like I've arrived at the After Party,' said the Decider.

'Not today.. Not like this,' sobbed Lottie.

'Lottie,' said the Decider. 'You know what this means.'

Lottie shook her head and spluttered on more tears; the praise that had once swam in her veins had gone baron.

'Your party is over. The hosts have deemed that your daily shows and daily parties are the least popular.'

'Just let me go. Let me get out of here.' Pleaded Lottie.

'As you know, there isn't enough air to give to this entire house. By virtue of the fans, you have been deemed the least resourceful star. Goodbye Lottie.'

First her screen went black. Then the green lights sunk into shadows. Finally she heard the hissing of air being sucked out from the walls. As her lungs scorched and writhed, Lottie gasped desperately at the floor. She distantly heard the sound of pounding and imagined that someone was breaking down the door to rescue her. In her last waking moments she realised that it was the sound of Lexi dancing from above.

Printed in Great Britain
by Amazon

20212730R00084